MY MANY COLORED DAYS

By **Dr. Seuss**

PAINTINGS BY
STEVE JOHNSON and **LOU FANCHER**

ALFRED A. KNOPF   NEW YORK

Some days are yellow.

Some are blue.

On different days
I'm different too.

You'd be
surprised
how many ways

I change
on Different
Colored
Days.

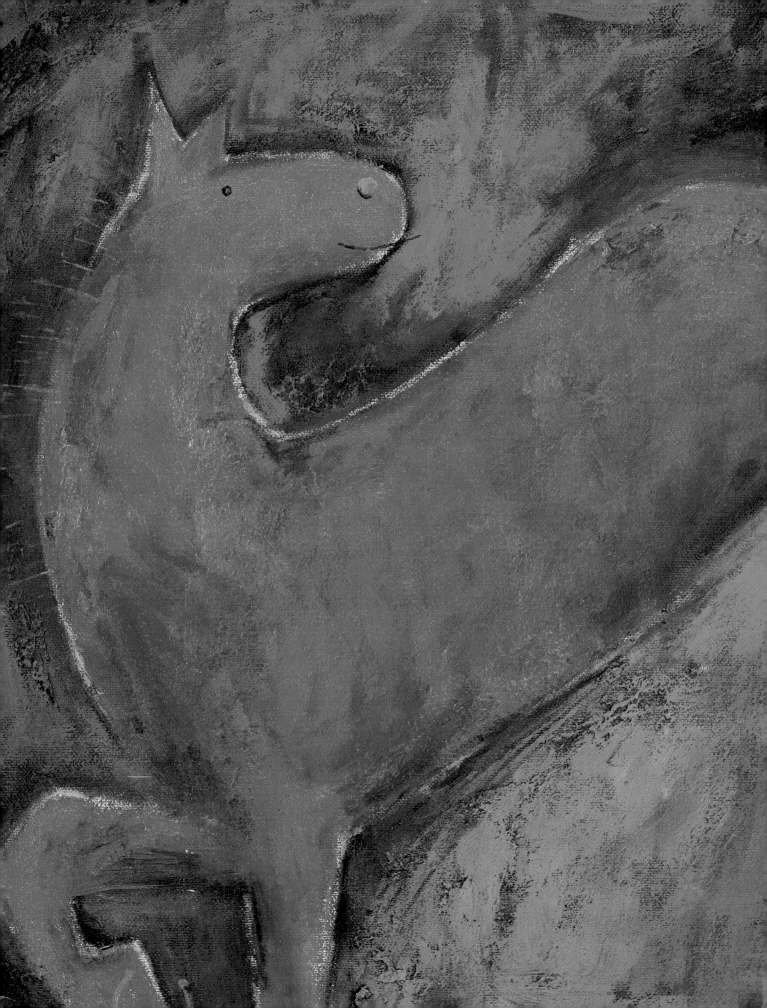

On Bright Red Days
how **good** it feels
to be a horse
and **kick** my heels!

On other days I'm other things.

On Bright Blue Days

I flap my wings.

Some days, of course,
feel sort of Brown.

Then I feel slow
and  low,

low

Then comes a Yellow Day.

And,

WHEEEEE

I am a busy, b^uzzy bee.

Gray Day . . . Everything is gray.

I watch. But nothing moves today.

Then
all of a sudden

I'm a

circus seal!

On my Orange Days
that's how I feel.

Green Days. Deep deep in the sea.

Cool and quiet **fish. That's me.**

On Purple Days

I'm sad.

I groan.

I drag my tail.

I walk alone.

But when my days are Happy

Pink

it's great to jump
and just not think.

Then come my Black Days.
MAD. And
loud.
I howl.
I growl at every cloud.

Then comes a Mixed-Up Day.

And **WHAM !**

I don't know **wHo**
or **WHat**
I am!

**But it all
turns out all right,
you see.**

And I go back
to being . . .

me.

To Ted, who colored my days...and my life.

—Audrey Geisel

For Denise and Frances.

—Steve Johnson and Lou Fancher

THIS IS A BORZOI BOOK PUBLISHED BY ALFRED A. KNOPF

www.randomhouse.com/kids

Educators and librarians, for a variety of teaching tools, visit us at
www.randomhouse.com/teachers

Library of Congress Cataloging-in-Publication Data
Seuss, Dr.
My many colored days / by Dr. Seuss ; illustrated by Steve Johnson and Lou Fancher.
p. cm.
SUMMARY: This rhyming story describes each day in terms of a particular color which in turn is associated with specific emotions.
ISBN-10: 0-679-87597-2 (trade) — ISBN-10: 0-679-97597-7 (lib. bdg.)
ISBN-13: 978-0-679-87597-0 (trade) — ISBN-13: 978-0-679-97597-7 (lib. bdg.)
[1. Color—Fiction. 2. Day—Fiction. 3. Emotions—Fiction. 4. Stories in rhyme.]
I. Johnson, Steve, ill. II. Fancher, Lou, ill. III. Title.
PZ8.3.G276My 1996
[E]—dc20
95-18893

Book design by Lou Fancher

Printed in China

27 26 25 24